Dear Parent:

Buckle up! You are about to join your child on a very exciting journey. The destination? Independent reading!

Road to Reading will help you and your child get there. The program offers books at five levels, or Miles, that accompany children from their first attempts at reading to successfully reading on their own. Each Mile is paved with engaging stories and delightful artwork.

Getting Started
For children who know the alphabet and are eager to begin reading
• easy words   • fun rhythms   • big type   • picture clues

Reading With Help
For children who recognize some words and sound out others with help
• short sentences   • pattern stories   • simple plotlines

Reading On Your Own
For children who are ready to read easy stories by themselves
• longer sentences   • more complex plotlines   • easy dialogue

First Chapter Books
For children who want to take the plunge into chapter books
• bite-size chapters   • short paragraphs   • full-color art

Chapter Books
For children who are comfortable reading independently
• longer chapters   • occasional black-and-white illustrations

There's no need to hurry through the Miles. Road to Reading is designed without age or grade levels. Children can progress at their own speed, developing confidence and pride in their reading ability no matter what their age or grade.

So sit back and enjoy the ride—every Mile of the way!

For Anne, my very dear friend
who is our brightest and
most spirited star
J.P.

Library of Congress Cataloging-in-Publication Data
Brown, Margaret Wise, 1910-1952.
I like stars / by Margaret Wise Brown ; illustrated by Joan Paley.
   p.   cm. — (Road to reading. Mile 1)
Summary: A simple poem describing all kinds of stars that appear in the night sky.
ISBN 0-307-26105-0 (pbk.)
1. Stars—Juvenile poetry. 2. Children's poetry, American. [1. Stars—Poetry.
2. American poetry.] I. Paley, Joan, ill. II. Title. III. Series.
PS3503. R82184I16 1998
811'.52—dc21   98-12015
                                                                CIP
                                                                AC

A GOLDEN BOOK • New York
Golden Books Publishing Company, Inc.
New York, New York 10106

ISBN: 0-307-26105-0

                                                    A MCMXCVIII

I Like Stars

by Margaret Wise Brown
illustrated by Joan Paley

with an afterword by Leonard S. Marcus

I like stars.

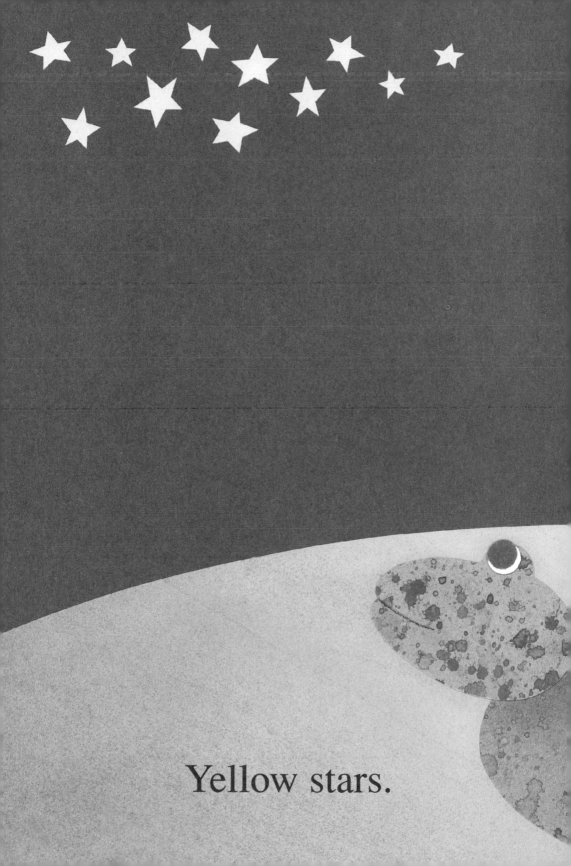

Yellow stars.

Green stars.

Red stars.

Blue stars.

I like stars.

Far stars.

Quiet stars.

Bright stars.

Light stars.

I like stars.

A star that is
shooting across
the dark sky.

A star that is shining

right straight in your eye.

I like stars.

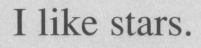

About the Author

Margaret Wise Brown liked stars.

As a girl she liked to sleep on the upstairs porch in the summer with her sister and their cat named Ole King Cole. From her bed she could look out over the trees at the stars.

Could it be that on one of those warm summer nights Margaret was thinking about "a star that is shining right straight in your eye"?

Gazing up at the stars and moon put Margaret in a dreamy mood. What a mystery it all was!

Years later, as a grown-up, she still enjoyed looking up at the night sky—and letting her mind wander.

One night she fell asleep at her window. The next morning she awoke and wrote down the words in her head: "Goodnight moon. . . goodnight stars. . ." Those words became her best-known book, *Goodnight Moon.*

As a famous author, she liked to tell her friends that she did not actually write books. She "dreamt" them.

Sometimes, it seems, she really did!

In *I Like Stars*, Margaret Wise Brown tells about many different kinds of stars: blue stars, green stars, quiet ones, bright ones.

What kinds of stars do *you* see when you look up at the stars at night?

—*Leonard S. Marcus*

Leonard S. Marcus is a well-known biographer and historian, and the author of Margaret Wise Brown: Awakened by the Moon.